Dream, Little One, Dream!

Written by Chimere R. McLean

Illustrated by Neel Solanki

To Cameron:

You are the light of my life.
May all your dreams come true.

-Mommy

Bedtime is my favorite time.

After laughing and playing all day,

1

I say my prayers
and close
my eyes.

Then, I am
taken
away...

2

...to lands of
fairies and
butterflies
of happiness
and glee.

Their wings
flutter and
tickle my
nose both
magical and
free.

The unicorn gives me a ride through fields filled with lilies so white, where bunnies and puppies frolic all day and crickets chirp through the night.

I follow the deer to the river.

Happily, we play on the shore,

I play with the dolphins in the ocean so blue

and swim with the mermaids so fair.

Then, I am taken up by the Pegasus.

Its wings help us

glide through the air.

The Pegasus and I soar through the sky, and I am warmed by the light of the sun.

Joined by the birds we fly in a "V", and I think, *I've never known such fun!*

13

A hurricane of
stars, from the
heavens above,
flows down from
the clouds as I'm
showered with
love.

This journey has left me weary and weak,
but there's no need for a bed
or counting sheep.

I gently lie down
     on cotton-like clouds,
          and the angels sing me to sleep.

16

My adventure,
it seems,
has come
to an end,
but your
dream,
little one,
has yet
to begin.

17

So, say your prayers, close your eyes, and dream, little one, dream!

ABOUT THE AUTHOR

Chimere R. McLean has worked as an educator in Delaware public schools for the past 15 years. She resides in Middletown, Delaware with her husband, Chris, and son, Cameron. She was inspired by the lack of diversity in the children's books she read to her son and is dedicated to providing opportunities for all children to see themselves as the main character in a story. Although, *Dream, Little One, Dream!* is the author's first venture into writing children's books, you can look forward to seeing more from this author in the future.

Made in the USA
Middletown, DE
23 November 2018